A WORD TO PARENTS AND TEACHERS

This book is about you, and me, and all others who try to get along with one another. It is especially written for those who follow Christ, for above all others, we should learn to live together happily. If we who are believers are all friends of Jesus—having been changed into new people through Him— then we ought to be friends with one another.

So don't be tempted to stop with a story about Squire Squirrel, Oscar Owl, and their friends. There is much more here for you and your child. After you and your child have read the story through several times to capture its meaning, talk with him or her about the questions at the end of this book. They will point to some important guidelines in the interpersonal relationships of believers.

Printed in the United States of America

THE HOUSE IN THE HOLE IN THE SIDE OF THE TREE

by V. Gilbert Beers

Illustrated by Jan Jones

© 1973 by V. Gilbert Beers

Library of Congress Catalog Number: 72-13629

ISBN: 0-8024-3599-8

MOODY PRESS • CHICAGO

"Welllll, what do YOU want?" Squire Squirrel growled. He looked so angry that the Chipmunk Twins almost ran away.

"We . . . uh . . . that is, do you have a hammer that we can borrow?" they answered, almost whispering.

"NO!" shouted Squire Squirrel. "What do you think this is, a hardware store?" Then he slammed the door so hard that the tree shook. And his house in the hole in the side of the tree shook, too.

Squire mumbled and grumbled all the way up the stairs. He looked around his house to be sure that it was all right. He had not made the house very well. He knew that he must stop slamming doors, or the whole house would fall down.

"I really should build a better house in a better place," Squire grumbled to himself. "These neighbors never do anything for me. All they ever do is borrow hammers and things." Of course, Squire Squirrel never thought to ask himself what he did for his neighbors.

Just then, Squire heard something at
his window.

"YOO-WHOOO!" someone said.

Squire opened his window and stared
into the face of Oscar Owl, sitting
on a big limb of a big tree.

"Nosey neighbors!" Squire mumbled.
"They're even sitting in trees outside
my window. What do YOU want, Oscar?"

"What do I want?" Oscar began to think.
"Yes, what DO I want? I seem to have
forgotten. I know that I was to remember
not to forget something. But now I've
forgotten what I was supposed to
remember not to forget."

"I suppose you want to borrow something, too," Squire shouted.

"Why, yes, of course," said Oscar. "How thoughtful of you to remember. But what was I to borrow? Let me think. Oh, yes, I need a steasuring mick. Oh, dear, no, I mean a measuring stick."

Squire slammed his window so hard that a board fell from his house in the hole in the side of the tree. "If I had a measuring stick, I'd wrap it around his silly neck," Squire grumbled.

Squire flopped down in a big chair.
It was very quiet now in the house.
He thought for a moment that it would
be nice to have some friends. But just
as he started to think that, he heard
a noise outside.

BANG! BANG! CRASH! BANG!

Squire ran to the window and opened
it wide. He could not see anything
special, but he could still hear
that noise.

Then Squire shouted as loud as he
could, "WILL YOU BE QUIET!" Of course,
Squire didn't know that he was making
more noise than the noise was making.

Squire had just slammed the window shut when he heard someone knocking on the door downstairs. When he opened it, there were his next-tree neighbors, smiling and looking like very happy squirrels.

"Do you have a saw that we could bor . . ." they started to say. But Squire slammed the door without bothering to answer.

That night, Squire lay in his bed for
a long time, looking up at the big
moon over his next-tree neighbors'
tree. He felt very lonely. And he
felt very sad.

Squire knew that he really wanted
some friends. But he knew that he would
never have friends by slamming doors
and windows and shouting when they
tried to be friendly. With these
thoughts running through his mind,
Squire fell asleep.

While he slept, Squire dreamed that a hammer and a saw were chasing him. He ran to each neighbor's house to ask for help. But each time he tried to talk, someone slammed a door or window.

At last, the hammer and saw chased him all the way home. As he locked himself in his house, Squire felt more lonely and sad than he had ever felt. Then he sat down and cried. But there was no friend to help him feel better.

The next morning Squire woke up suddenly. Someone was knocking on his door. He ran down the steps and opened the door.

Squire almost expected to see the big hammer and saw standing there, ready to chase him again. But instead, he saw all his neighbors, laughing and looking very happy.

Squire started to ask, "Well, what do YOU want?" But he didn't. Then he started to slam the door. But he didn't. He kept thinking about his dream. He knew now how it felt to have someone slam a door when you come to see him.

Squire was happy that a hammer and saw were not chasing him now. He was very happy that his neighbors were not slamming doors. And he was very, very happy that they had come to see him.

"Will you come in?" Squire asked. "Will you have breakfast with me?"

"Later!" they all shouted cheerfully. "Come with us! We have a surprise for you!"

Then Squire's neighbors took him to
a big tree not far away. In the side
of the big tree there was a big hole.
And in the big hole was a beautiful
new house.

"It's your new house," they all shouted.
"We made it for you because we like
you and want to be your friends."
Squire Squirrel was so ashamed that
he could not even look at his wonderful
neighbors. While he had been shouting
at them and slamming doors and windows,
they had been making a house for him.

"I'm sorry that I've been so grumpy,"
he said. "I'll never slam a door or
window again when you come to see me."

"Dear me," said Oscar the Owl. "I
seem to have forgotten to remember
that you slammed doors and windows."

The Chipmunk Twins began to laugh.
Then the next-tree neighbors, who
weren't next-tree neighbors anymore,
began to laugh, too. Even Squire
Squirrel began to laugh. Then all the
friends went inside to look at Squire's
new house in the hole in the side of
the tree.

SOMETHING TO TALK ABOUT

1. Why should Jesus' friends be friends with each other? Read I
John 4:11. Can we tell Jesus that we really love Him if we do not
love His friends? Read also I John 4: 12, 20.

2. What did Squire's neighbors do for him? Why did they do
something special for him? Should we do special things for others
who are Jesus' friends? Should we do special things for others who
do not like us? Read I John 3: 18 and Galatians 6: 9.

3. What would have happened if Squire's neighbors had treated
him the way he treated them? Is it better to treat others the way
they treat us, or the way we want them to treat us? Read Matthew
7: 12 and Luke 6: 31. What does the Bible say?

4. What did Jesus do to those who hurt him? How does He want
us to treat those who hurt us? Read Matthew 5: 43-47. How does
He want us to treat His friends? Read Romans 12: 10 and I Thes-
salonians 4: 9.